Swan River

THE PAINTED DAISIES PREQUEL

LJ EVANS

Swan River

The Painted Daisies Prequel

By LJ Evans

This book is a work of fiction. While reference might be made to actual historical events or existing people and locations, the events, names, characters, places, and incidents are either the product of the author's imagination or are used fictitiously, and any resemblance to actual persons, living or dead, business establishments, events, or locales is entirely coincidental.

SWAN RIVER © 2022 by LJ Evans

LJ Evans Books

www.ljevansbooks.com

Cover Design: ©River Briar Designs
Cover Photos: © iStock NAGAETS.jr, Vidok | Depositphotos eskaylim
Content & Line Editor: Evans Editing
Copy Editor: Jenn Lockwood Editing Services
Proofing: Karen Hrdlicka

Published in the United States

Message for the Reader

Swan River is a PREQUEL that gives you the inside scoop into the lives of The Painted Daisies band members on the day Landry Kim was murdered, including Landry herself.

This little novella overlaps in timeline with the beginning of book one, *Sweet Memory*, but in *Sweet Memory* the full Paisley and Jonas love story is explored, and it has a happily ever after that doesn't take place here.

This prequel ends on a cliffhanger. But the series is now complete and ready to be binged.

Keep reading for a sneak peek at the secrets and dangers hovering around each of the band members and see if you can figure out who murdered Landry before the band and their team do. Then, dive into each of the stories to find out all the juicy secrets.

Playlist

https://spoti.fi/39x2ELD

Chapter One

Paisley

RUN TO YOU
Performed by Lea Michele

Paisley lifted her head from the keyboard after she finished the song and was surprised to find the recording studio completely silent. The air held a strange vibration as if the chords were still traveling through the room. A sea of eyes stared at her. Landry's face came into focus first before Jonas's gaze caught her attention through the glass. There was a mix of pride and awe in both their expressions, and it filled Paisley's chest until it almost burst.

They were good. The songs were really, really good.

She felt it all the way down into the depths of her soul. Paisley had been scribbling away on napkins, notebooks, and school papers long before Landry had formed The Painted Daisies with her friends. And even though this was the band's third album, even though they'd been playing to sold-out stadiums and the music critics had been sending accolades their way, nothing had felt like these songs. Nothing.

Paisley's gaze shot to where Jonas stood by the mixing console. Her insides leaped, and her pulse thrummed as if Adria was still pounding away on her drums. She wished it was just the two of them—her and Jonas—sitting behind her keys so he could kiss her. So he could wrap his arms around her and prove the truth of her words. That love was the only truly meaningful part of humanity's existence.

Jonas's face broke into a huge smile. He shoved a hand through his dark-blond waves, and then, he put his palm to the glass, fingers wide. Her heart squeezed tight with pleasure and joy. It was as if she could feel the pressure of his hand on her chest where it had lain multiple times as he listened to the rhythm of her heartbeat. If there hadn't been an entire room between them, she would have met his palm with hers and let the emotions of the songs fill the space between them with the sense of coming home.

"Holy shit, Paise!" Landry's voice broke the quiet that had settled over all of them, drawing Paisley's eyes back to her sister. Even though she could hear the admiration in Landry's gritty tone, guilt swarmed through her at the hurt on Landry's face. Paisley had never finished any of their music on her own before. She'd never gotten all the way to playing them for the band without her sister having had a say in them.

Except…she hadn't been alone with these songs either. She just hadn't been with Landry.

"We'll have to move everything around," Landry said, tapping the rings on each of her middle fingers together in thought. Her overly round eyes narrowed, and she twisted her long black hair as she considered the handwritten track list scrawled on the whiteboard that she and Brady had been agonizing over.

Fiadh bounced over to Paisley with her dark-red curls spinning about her. She slung her arm around Paisley's shoulders.

"Little Bit, love sounds good on you!" Fiadh laughed, her amber eyes sparkling. Paisley felt her skin flush as she shot a glance at Jonas in the control room. Relief settled through her when she realized Jonas hadn't heard. Instead, he was deep in discussion with studio owner—country-rock legend, Brady O'Neil.

"She's right," Leya said, finger resting on the cleft in her chin as her brown eyes darted to Landry who was still assessing the album's tracklist. "These are your best songs yet. You and Landry outdid yourselves."

Landry whipped around to face them. "I had nothing to do with them. They're all Paisley."

Maybe it was just Paisley's guilty conscience that heard the quiet rebuke in her sister's tone, but she didn't think so. Tension had been growing between them ever since they'd arrived in Grand Orchard and Paisley had gone on her first date with Jonas.

Sensing the friction and wanting to soothe it as always, Adria twirled her sticks and climbed out from behind her drums with model-like grace to tuck her arm through Landry's. Her bright-blue eyes flickered to Paisley with a slight frown, but it was Nikki who actually spoke.

"Love is in the air, Lan. Get ready for a whole slew of new songs."

Nikki's tease sent Paisley's heart into overdrive, and she shot yet another glance toward the glass. Her stomach flipped because it was obvious Jonas had heard this time. His grin grew, and he winked at Paisley—a damn wink that said *I told you so*. A wink that should have annoyed her but really just made her melt inside until she was nothing more than a boiling pot of desire.

Brady strode into the room, excitement radiating from his face. "Okay, with the first song, I think we should start with just Paisley's voice. Then, after the second measure, I want Adria to come in on a gentle beat with the tom-toms. Every two measures, we'll add another instrument. Leya's sitar, followed by Fiadh's banjo, then Landry and Nikki on guitar before Paisley finally joins in on the keyboard. Do we want to try it or just start laying tracks?"

It was Fee who laughed and replied, "I think we should try it a few times together before we start recording anything."

He shrugged, "Sometimes, just going with it is better than anything you could plan."

While everyone went to grab their instruments, Paisley shot another smile in Jonas's direction. Landry stepped in front of her, breaking her view.

"Are you really just going to forget everything that happened yesterday?" Landry whispered, her disappointment pounding through each syllable.

Paisley's heart grew heavy. She hated that being with Jonas was causing a rift between them. Landry was the one person she admired most in this world. The person responsible for everything Paisley was and hoped to become. But she also didn't understand how Landry could see how happy she was with Jonas and still want her to give him up.

So, instead of replying with words they'd both regret, she turned back to the music and the suggestions Brady had made.

♫ ♫ ♫

Paisley's voice was scratchy by the time she came out of the iso booth hours later. She was surprised to find their manager Tommy had been joined by their label owner, Nick Jackson. Nick hadn't shown up for a recording since their first album, and she wondered what had dragged him all the way from New York City. Whereas Tommy looked like an aging rock star, Nick looked like a banker in a perfectly pressed gray suit with short brown hair that was graying at the temples and a clean-shaven square jaw.

The two men were in deep discussion with Brady about the new songs and the track order. While all the daisies had input, it was Landry who'd always had the innate sense of what it would take to make each song, album, and show a success. The band trusted her final decisions implicitly. She was the fire that fueled them. The force who'd first propelled them into existence and then launched them into worldwide fame once Lost Heart Records had come onboard.

Landry joined them, her lean frame with small curves that matched Paisley's almost vibrating with excitement. If it wasn't for their seven-inch height difference, her and her sister could be twins. They had the same large brown eyes, high cheekbones, oval faces, and straight black hair as their Korean mother.

Watching her sister in action was usually impressive, but today it only made her knotted stomach twist more. She wished again that finding the one person who made her feel whole wasn't causing a rift between her and Landry.

As if reading her mind, Jonas appeared at her side, offering a gentle smile along with the cup of tea he'd brought to soothe her achy vocal cords. Before he'd entered her world, all Paisley had wanted to do after a day of recording was find a quiet space where silence would be her only companion. But now, all she wanted was to lose herself in Jonas.

"You ready to get out of here for a while?" Jonas asked.

Paisley nodded, and Jonas hooked his pinky with hers, joining them together. When she looked down at them, she could see how different they were in size and shape and color, and yet it felt as if they were perfect this way—with his enormous hand dwarfing hers. Just like how the brown and green of their eyes blended perfectly. They were her song come to life.

"Where are you going?" Landry's voice halted them near the door.

"To Jonas's," Paisley said, not quite meeting her sister's eye.

"Nikki's stepmom is here, and Ronan and his crew will be at the farmhouse at eight for the bonfire. I need your help setting up," Landry said, the admonishment ringing through her words as she took in Paisley's fingers twisted with Jonas's.

Jonas bristled, shoulders going back, and Paisley knew he was mere moments from exploding again. She couldn't handle it right now. She was too exhausted from the hours she'd been at the keyboard and still too battered and bruised from the harsh words that had gone unforgiven between her and

Landry.

"I know. We'll be there," Paisley promised.

Landry left the men, crossed the room, and lowered her voice so the others couldn't hear her.

"Maybe it would be better if Jonas didn't come," Landry said quietly. "We'd hate for him to hit one of the film crew if they accidentally said something wrong."

"Lan!" Paisley exclaimed right as Jonas growled, "Fuck you."

Landry just glared, as if his outburst proved her point.

"At least I actually *want* to make Paisley happy," Jonas said, voice dark with emotions he was trying to hold back.

Landry stepped even closer until she was almost nose-to-nose with Jonas. "What the hell are you insinuating?"

"I don't think I need to spell it out for you," Jonas snapped.

"Stop!" Paisley cried. She loved that they were both trying to protect her in their own way, but it only made the chasm between them widen further. "This isn't helping. We need to talk. All of us. But not today. Not now, when everyone's tempers are still high."

She pushed Jonas in the chest so he moved backward toward the door. She could hear the tapping of Landry's rings banging out her frustration and worry behind her, but she didn't turn around. She just headed for the exit with Jonas.

"I refuse to let you ruin your life with one wrong decision, Paisley," her sister's voice followed them.

Her grief turned to burning hurt and anger as Landry's words hit every single sore spot in her soul. She'd almost forgiven Landry for the words said in the heat of the moment the day before about her decision-making. But today, they were so much worse because Landry knew what she was saying, knew how they'd make her feel, and she'd still said them.

Paisley dropped Jonas's hand and spun around. "Wrong decision?! How could you, Lan? Just because my decision isn't the one that makes your life easier, doesn't mean it's wrong. I know what makes me happy. I know who I want at my side, and if you don't like it, then you don't have to be a part of it."

Landry's eyes widened at Paisley's passion as much as at the words. Paisley regretted them instantly, wishing she could take them back, but she wouldn't, not with Landry still shooting venomous looks in Jonas's direction.

"Paise," she said, her tone only slightly regretful. "You don't understand."

"No. *You* don't understand. Because Mom is right, you've never cared for anything more than you've cared for this band. Stay out of my personal life! You no longer have a say in it."

Then, Paisley turned on her heel and stormed out with Jonas right behind her. As soon as the door of the studio slammed shut, the bitter remorse building inside her escaped in a quiet sob. Paisley had never struck out at Landry that way before, and it hurt. It had stung not only Landry but Paisley too. She didn't want her sister out of her life in any way, shape, or form. But how could Landry not see all the good that Paisley saw in Jonas? The gentle heart and protective soul? How he wanted the very best for her just like Landry did?

Jonas caught up to her, pulling Paisley into his chest and wrapping a muscled arm around her. He kissed the top of her head.

"Paisley, I'm sorry," he said, knowing he'd pushed when she'd wanted to run. But maybe that was the problem. Maybe she'd been running and hiding for so long that no one else knew how to see her as anything but the person in the shadows.

Paisley rested her forehead against his chest, arms going around his waist as he tugged her closer, the husky male scent of him filling her senses and making her feel safe and warm. She lifted her chin, stood on her tiptoes, and pulled his face toward hers, letting their lips touch as she'd been longing to do since she'd first played their love song for the band hours earlier.

The moment their mouths touched her veins flooded with heat. This was no slow build, just a complete and utter longing that raged through her. Desire so strong she forgot everything except how good it felt to have their bodies aligned with his soul calling to hers. At first, Jonas barely returned her kiss, but when she darted a tongue along his seam, he let out a guttural groan before devouring her completely. Lips and teeth and tongue battled with hers as if trying to own her in some deeply primitive way that Paisley should have hated but only loved.

A loud cough interrupted their fiery embrace, followed by her bodyguard saying, "Perhaps we should take this inside, away from any potential cameras."

Paisley's eyes opened to find Jonas's filled with more regret. If their heated kiss ended up on some website—or worse, in another scary note—it would be just one more thing for him to feel sorry about.

But this hadn't been his fault. This had been all her. She gave Jonas a soft smile and said, "Sorry I attacked you in broad daylight on the street."

He didn't return the smile. Instead, his eyes darted around, as if searching for the asshole photographer, or the stalker, or both. She grabbed his hand and tugged him in the direction of his apartment. She needed to be alone with him. She needed to fill herself with the sense of belonging, of being seen, of being adored that only Jonas had ever given her. And this time, she didn't want it to end until they'd lost every single article of clothing and twined themselves together from head to toe in the closest way possible.

She wanted this. She wanted him. No…she *needed* him. Like the dark needed the sun to push away the shadows. It was time they gave in and found the crescendo that had been waiting for them for years.

Chapter Two

Leya

ALMOST HOME
Performed by Mariah Carey

Just like everyone else in the room, Leya was trying not to watch the little showdown going on by the door. It wasn't Landry holding herself tightly back with anger that surprised her. After all, Landry was always the first into every battle, defending them personally or the band as a whole. Instead, it was the fury on Paisley's face that had the entire band holding their breath.

They'd never seen Paisley stand up to Landry like this. Just the night before, Leya had told Landry she was trying too hard to protect Paisley from heartache, even if it was heartache coming from a boy with an iffy past and a violent streak. But she'd gone all Landry, refusing to give in. Refusing to let any of them be hurt on her watch.

Nikki joined her, adjusting the sloppy bun she'd wrapped her long strands in that morning. Every day, Nikki threatened to cut it all off, and every day, each of them talked her out of it. It wasn't just because it bonded them in some strange way for all of them but Fee to have black hair. It was because everyone knew Nikki would regret it if she did. The long hair suited her almost more than any of them, and when she left it in her natural, onyx curls, it was even more stunning.

Their first album cover had played up their similarities.

They'd all worn white leather jackets with their backs to the camera. Only Paisley, who was over half a foot shorter than the rest of them, and Fiadh, with her deep-red hair, had stood out. The rest could only be told apart by the daisies emblazoned on their jackets. It had been their manager's idea to emphasize the band's name by having them choose a favorite daisy to be etched and painted onto their instruments, mic stands, and clothes until the flowers had become almost synonymous with their names.

"Wow, I didn't think Little Bit actually had it in her," Nikki said quietly.

Leya nodded as Adria joined them, twirling her sticks unconsciously. Concern filled the air around them as they watched the sisters argue like they never had before. The tension growing between them was why the album had been struggling.

Paisley slammed her way out of the studio with Jonas hot on her trail, and Landry's shoulders slumped. She rubbed her fingers into her forehead and then turned to face them.

"Don't," Landry hissed before any of them could even breathe a word.

"I warned you." It was Adria who dared to voice Leya's thoughts aloud.

"I said don't," Landry growled. The emotions in her voice made it husky, dropping until it sounded like a wounded animal.

Fiadh bounced over to Landry and slung an arm around her. "Lan, it's going to be okay. She's just the first one of us to fall head over heels in love—so much so that she can't live without him. It's going to happen to all of us at some point."

"Lust isn't love." The words slipped out of Leya before she could take them back, and she instantly regretted them when her friends' faces spun to hers.

Nikki chuckled. "Better not let the documentary crew hear you say that tonight. We make our bread and butter on passion and sin."

Leya rolled her eyes. They knew how she felt about people's misconceptions that lust was love.

"I don't trust him. You didn't see how he went off yesterday on that photographer," Landry said.

"We're all on edge," Adria said quietly, and Leya's stomach turned, thinking of the gruesome notes with their faces scratched out that had caused their security team to double overnight and the FBI to show up in force.

"Hell, I almost lost it the other day, remember?" Fiadh said.

"You didn't, though," Landry grunted out. Silence surrounded them except for Landry's rings tapping together with her hands held prayer style. "It isn't just his anger that worries me. What happens when we leave?"

Leya knew exactly what Landry meant. If Paisley had convinced herself that what she felt was love, and then it all fell apart, she'd have a broken heart. One her sister wanted to protect her from.

"Trying to protect her before it happens isn't going to help. And who knows, maybe it will last," Nikki said.

Landry scoffed. "They're not even twenty. What the hell do they know about forever?"

"You're only five and half years older than her, Lan," Fee said.

"Exactly, and there's no way I could make a permanent relationship work."

"You're not her, Lan," Adria said. "Just because it isn't what you want or need, doesn't mean it isn't right for Little Bit."

Landry groaned and headed for the door. "I'm going for a run around the pond to clear my head before Ronan's crew and Nikki's mom shows up. I'll meet you back at the farmhouse."

As Landry and her bodyguard disappeared through the studio door, Leya's phone rang. It was with a twist of pleasure and dread that she saw her mother's face on the screen. Her parents were concerned about what was happening with the creepy notes. While they seemed aimed at Jonas and Paisley rather than just the band, no one was sure. Not with the hate group, For Greater Tomorrows, spewing gross rhetoric toward her dad and their entire family in an attempt to sway the public away from the Matherton-Singh ticket.

When Leya had first joined the Daisies in high school, everyone in her family, including Leya, had thought it would be temporary. It had been a way for her to honor her grandmother and the Indian instruments *Nani* had taught her to play. But then it had become home…a place for her to truly be herself in a way she rarely was around her genius family.

"Mom," Leya answered, drifting over to the side of the room for a bit of privacy.

"Leya, we need you here." Her mother's voice was firm and demanding, whereas her father's would have been soft and cajoling.

"I'll be there tomorrow night, just like we planned," Leya said with a confused frown. She was going even if she was dreading putting on a suit and closed-toe pumps and wearing a somber face.

"The plan was to have you here for your father's acceptance speech, but now we need you earlier for interviews with the entire family."

"I can't come tonight, Mom. The documentary crew is shooting some final scenes," Leya reminded her.

Her mom huffed. "It isn't even being released until January, with the album, right? This is happening right now. We can't put this off."

She sighed. Even though her mother didn't understand Leya's career choice, she'd never asked her to quit. Not even when it could have been a detriment to her dad's political career. They'd just asked to see and be able to veto any marketing or publicity beforehand. What none of them had predicted was for the success and attention her dad had garnered in his first six years in Washington D.C. to lead to a nomination for vice president.

When she didn't say anything, her mom pushed. "This is important, Leya. We need you. I've arranged for a helicopter to pick you up."

Her family rarely asked her to be there anymore, so denying them this made her stomach twist. And the truth was, she was really proud of her dad. She was proud of all her family. Her mother and brother were saving lives with their surgical knives and her Dad had the chance to change the world. To truly make a difference.

"Fine. I'll come," Leya said, giving in while grimacing at the thought of telling an already upset Landry she was bailing on the filming tonight.

"Thank you." Her mom's voice was filled with relief, and Leya knew she'd made the right decision. "The helicopter will be at Grand Orchard General Hospital in thirty minutes."

"Okay, I'll see you soon."

In her normal fashion, her mom hung up without saying goodbye.

Leya turned around to where Adria, Nikki, and Fiadh were still in deep discussion about Landry and Paisley's blowup and the boy who was coming between them all. Leya's chest hurt at the thought of leaving them like this, but at least Nikki would be there—the peacemaker of their little group.

Leya joined her friends and said, "I'm not going to make the bonfire."

"What?" Fee demanded.

"Dad needs me at the convention earlier than planned."

"Maybe we should just reschedule the entire thing," Adria sighed. "We don't want them filming Landry and Paisley going at it again."

Leya felt torn in a way she'd never been before between her family and her friends. Remorse and worry filtered through her, and Nikki seemed to read it, saying, "Go be with your family, Leya. We'll figure this out."

Fiadh looked like she was going to protest again, but the look Nikki sent her had her closing her mouth. Leya wrapped her arms around Fee, but held them open and waved the other two women into her embrace. The four of them hugged, and Leya whispered into their ears, "Make sure they remember how much they love each other."

Then, she let them all go and walked out the door of the studio with two of the security detail following her onto the street. One of them was a Secret Service agent who'd joined her with her dad's bid for Vice President. Holden Kent was a tall wall of muscles who screamed typical American boy—everything Leya had never been attracted to—and yet, for some ungodly reason, her body seemed to not agree.

This made Leya extra prickly with him. She hated the way her nerve endings tingled whenever he was close, but she refused to give in to his magnetic lure. Not that he'd even think twice about kissing her the way she sometimes found him doing in her dreams. He'd never once sent her a look that was anything but professional.

Holden turned to the other bodyguard. "Miss Singh and I are taking a helicopter to the convention. The Secret Service will take over her protection. You won't be needed."

Her annoyance sparked even more, partly because he'd already known about the helicopter, but more because he was dismissing her security team without her okay or approval.

"I don't think so, Special Agent Kent. My team goes with me."

The dark-haired Garner bodyguard grimaced. "I don't think we can do more for you than the Secret Service. Let me just get Garner's okay to hand you off."

He pulled out his phone and stepped to the side of the

sidewalk while Leya glared at the agent. His face remained expressionless, except she could have sworn his lips twitched just a hair. There definitely was humor in his eyes when the Garner bodyguard came back and said, "I'll drive you both to the helicopter pad. Garner said to let him know when you're heading back so we can meet you."

Leya huffed, shouldered her bag, and headed for the SUV waiting for them on the street. While she hoped with every fiber of her being that her father and Guy Matherton would win the election, she also hoped they didn't, because she was already tired of having this cocky agent following her around. If they won, it would mean he'd be shadowing her for a lot longer than just a few months, and she wasn't sure her body could take it.

Chapter Three

Nikki

HOME
Performed by Foo Fighters

Nikki rubbed her temples, feeling the beginnings of a migraine coming on. It would be impossible to get through tonight with a film crew watching her if it kicked in as fiercely as the headaches sometimes did. She scrambled to her bag and pulled out her medicine.

She turned back to see Adria and Fiadh watching her with concern.

Their normally tight-knit group seemed to be full of drama these days. Once upon a time, they'd lived almost hip-to-hip, sharing rooms while touring with Watery Reflection, and even though they'd each had their own rooms on The Red Guitar tour, they'd still lived like sisters…Sisters she'd never had. The tension made her stomach clench and her chest tighten.

After downing her medicine, she turned to her friends and said, "I think Adria's right. We should reschedule the filming."

"You have a migraine?" Fee asked.

Nikki pushed against her temples again. "It might not develop into a full-blown one. I might have caught it early enough, but with Leya heading out and things being tense with Landry and Paisley, it seems better to postpone."

"I don't think the Hollywood Player Prince will agree. He's too used to getting his way," Adria said dryly.

Ronan Hawks was the documentary's creator and director. He'd made a name for himself filming edgy, dark music videos, including a couple for their Red Guitar album that had won awards. He was the epitome of a Hollywood narcissist and wouldn't be happy to have his budget or his schedule screwed up because of anything as ridiculous as a headache or family drama.

Nikki's phone buzzed, and she looked down to see Professor Maynard's name and number appear over the daisies on her lock screen. She forgot she'd agreed to meet with him this afternoon. He'd been so determined and so persistent ever since she'd arrived in Grand Orchard, and if she was truthful with herself, he'd dropped tantalizing hints that had been hard to ignore.

She could put him off. She should. In all likelihood, whatever he had to say would only increase the chances of her headache developing into a full-on throbbing monster refusing to be tamed. But she'd already postponed twice, each time doubting herself. Each time not wanting to know if her parents had kept things hidden from her all her life. Not little secrets either—life-altering ones.

The only good thing about the start of her headache was she could use it as an excuse to leave.

"I'm going to go get a coffee. Anyone want anything?" Nikki asked the others.

"No. Go take care of your headache before it turns into a beast. We'll call Ronan," Fiadh said, and Adria groaned, her distaste of the filmmaker clear. Fiadh smiled at her. "Safety in numbers, my friend."

Nikki left with her bodyguard in tow. She made her way past the charming old storefronts of downtown to the ivy-covered buildings that made up Wilson-Jacobs College. She'd been on campus only twice before, but she'd looked up Maynard's office on a site map that morning, so she knew the direction to head.

The university wasn't nearly as busy as it would be when the fall semester kicked in, but there were still students and faculty wandering the halls. When she reached the floor with Maynard's office, she turned to her bodyguard, Andy.

"I'd like you to wait here," she told him. She didn't want anyone listening to what the professor had to say because she wasn't sure she believed it.

Andy frowned, unhappy with this development, but didn't challenge her. Maybe it was because he knew, out of any of the Daisies, she was the one who'd had the most training in protecting herself. A lifetime of it at the hands of some of the best teachers. Not only her dad but his Green Beret friend and a host of martial arts instructors. Andy waited for her near the top of the stairs while she continued down several doors to Maynard's office.

She knocked and entered, only to freeze.

The office was a disaster—books had been tossed from the shelves, and the file cabinets were open with their contents spread along the floor. The two chairs in front of Maynard's large walnut desk had their cushions sliced open, while everything on the desktop had been thrown to the floor.

Professor Maynard was standing amidst the mess, laptop clutched to his chest and his trendy, black-framed glasses slipping down his nose. Anger and fear were etched over his face as his eyes found her in the doorway.

"Close the door!" he demanded.

She hesitated, but then did so, trying to find a spot to stand where she wouldn't be on top of his strewn belongings.

"Wh-what happened?" Nikki asked.

He looked at her with dark eyes that seemed to see through her and made a chill run up her spine. "You. You happened."

Nikki's mouth dropped open as fear curled through her.

"What are you talking about?"

The last time she'd met him, she'd thought he had a nice smile, which only added to his Indiana Jones appeal that she was sure made him popular with his students. Now, his glare made him look unhinged.

"They must know I'm close to the truth. They want what I found in L.A."

"Who's they?" Nikki asked, stomach clenching as the obvious truth finally hit her. His office had been ransacked by someone searching for something.

The office door crashed open, and Nikki jumped as another man burst into the room. He looked like the professor in many ways, but taller, lankier, rougher. As if he was accustomed to getting into bar fights. He even had a scar on his jaw that proved her thoughts. Dark, beady eyes took in the entire room before he stalked further into it and righted a chair that had been knocked over.

"What the hell?" the new man demanded.

"I must have tipped them off when I asked for the report on the shooting at the gas station," he told the other man, almost forgetting Nikki was there.

Her heart stopped and started. Was he talking about the gas station where her dad was killed? A wave of pain flew through her. It had been years since she'd lost him, but it sliced through her almost as if she was hearing about it for the first time.

The pounding in her head quadrupled.

"I told you, we needed to drop this entire stupid notion," the man with the scar growled. "Nothing good will come of it now. Nothing but death and destruction."

"I'm sorry. This was a mistake," Nikki said quietly, easing her way back toward the door and opening it.

The professor moved so fast it surprised her, slamming the door shut and grabbing her arm. At first, she recoiled, wishing she hadn't left her bodyguard, but then her training came back and with a swift movement, she'd batted his arm away and prepared for retaliation.

He jerked his hand back to his chest, pushing his glasses up and stepping away. "I'm sorry. It's just… It's important. Please. I have proof. I can show it to you."

She looked around the destroyed office.

"What proof?" the other man asked, face scrunching into a scowl.

"It's not here. I wouldn't be stupid enough to just leave it laying around," the professor insisted, and the other man's eyes squinted at the desperation in Maynard's voice.

Every alarm bell in Nikki's body was telling her to get the hell out of there.

"I…I think it's best if we just drop this," she said quietly, hand slowly moving toward the doorknob again.

"Please," the professor begged again. "Give me one more chance. We're so close to the truth. Closer than anyone has been in decades. My brother and I…we need this."

The two men exchanged a strange look that only increased the turmoil inside her. Nikki wanted to tell him to go to hell. She wanted to leave and never think about any of this again. But the little things Professor Maynard had told her about her family had all rung true in a way that seemed both impossible and probable at the same time.

If she had him come to the farmhouse tonight, there would be a host of bodyguards and her friends around. She'd be safe. She'd have to tell the band something or just let them assume she had thing for the attractive college professor.

"Tonight. At the farmhouse with everyone there. Any time after seven," she said before stepping through the door. "But only you, Professor. If you both show up, I won't be able to explain it."

"Thank you! You won't regret it," Professor Maynard called after her, relief coasting over his face, but his brother looked wary and thoughtful.

Nikki already regretted it. Regretted ever letting him close. Her stomach was in turmoil, and her head was now throbbing mercilessly, causing white lights to flicker through her vision. She needed to climb into bed, shut all the blinds, and sleep until it disappeared, and that was exactly what she was going to do.

She slipped out the door before either of the men could stop her again, found her way to her bodyguard, back through the college, and out to one of the SUVs that were waiting for the band outside the studio all the while doubts, fear, and pain trailed her.

As she went to get in the vehicle, her skin prickled, and she glanced up to see a man leaning up against the white pillar of the bakery across the street. His arms were crossed, showcasing forearms that were huge and bulging like the rest of him—black hair, hooded eyes, muscles, and tattoos that screamed of some ancient-Egyptian, godlike lineage. He was beautiful. She'd seen him that morning as well when they'd arrived at the studio. It should have frightened her. It should have been something she mentioned to the others, especially with the creepy notes arriving daily, but she hadn't. There was something almost mythical about him, as if she'd blink and he'd disappear.

As they started to drive away, she turned back and the man was gone, just like she'd expected. A mirage. A figment of her imagination.

She closed her eyes and rested her head on the seat back. The pain gripping her pushed everything else out of her mind. The fear. The doubts. Nothing remained but the knowledge that if she didn't lose herself to sleep, she'd never shake the agony swallowing her.

When she got to the early-twentieth-century mansion the locals called "The Farmhouse," the sun had started to fall below the mountains, casting the orchards around it into shadows. The house itself was silent with Landry out running and the others still in town. Silence was what she needed.

Nikki rushed up the stairs and down the hall to the sunny bedroom she'd claimed at the front of the house. Tonight, she needed darkness, so she drew the blinds and curtains, turning the room pitch black. She fumbled her way to the bed, stripping as she went, and slid into the cool sheets before resting her fevered brow on the pillowcase and letting herself drift away.

Chapter Four

Adria

HOME SWEET HOME
Performed by Mötley Crüe

"*Let me see if Tommy will* talk to Ronan for us," Fiadh said and headed across the studio to where their manager was in a fierce discussion with the owner of their record label. There was so much animosity floating around them this week, Adria wondered if Mercury was in retrograde.

Her stomach clenched tight at the thought of having to talk to Ronan Hawk. Her friends were confused by her active disklike of him these days when they'd flirted and teased for years. But the humiliation she'd experienced at his hands in January was burned into her brain, even if her body tried to forget it whenever he was near. She hated her natural reaction to him almost as much as he hated him.

Asshole.

Adria's phone rang, a classic The Mills song that had brought her and her dad's love of music together. Drum riffs that she'd practiced almost as soon as she'd picked up the sticks. She was surprised to get a call from him when he was supposed to be on his way to Colombia to see her mom.

"*¿Qué pasa, Papá?*" she asked.

"Thank God, you're okay!" *Papá's* deep voice came over the line, speaking fast in Spanish, full of relief and panic in a way she'd never heard before. It caused the tension in Adria's shoulders and abdomen to triple. "You need to get out of there. We're calling your detail now. We need you to go underground for a few days."

"What's going on?" Adria's heart slammed hard against her rib cage. Three security guards burst into the room at a run, drawing everyone's eyes and causing her pulse to leap.

"Your sister…she's been kidnapped," *Papá* told her. "The ransom has already come, and there are threats that you will be next if we don't pay."

"Wh-what?" Adria gasped as her hands froze around her twirling drumsticks.

Her father had been kidnapped in Colombia, but that had been two decades ago, and even though he was a constant target for the big-oil companies he went up against, there'd never been any threat to her or her siblings.

"We need to leave," the female security guard said as the three of them surrounded her.

"Adria, are they there?" *Papá* asked.

"Yes," she managed to breathe out.

"Go. Go with them now."

"Tati…" Emotions choked her voice, thinking of her somber little sister. Thinking of what they might do to her.

"We'll get her back, Adria. We will, but I can't focus on what I need to do for her while I'm worried about you as well. Go. Now."

"Okay…I'm going."

"Leave your phone," he commanded.

"What? No. How will I hear from you?"

"We'll get word through your team. Don't argue. Just go."

He hung up, and she stared at the phone with trepidation, fear, and sadness soaring through her. Fiadh was at her side in a flash, her normally happy face a furrow of frowns and worry.

"What's wrong?" Fiadh asked.

"Someone…" She couldn't even finish the sentence. Her heart was pounding too hard, fear taking over.

The female bodyguard spoke for her. "Someone has taken Ms. Rojas's sister, and they've threatened to come after her as well. We need to take her into hiding for a few days."

"Feck," Fee exclaimed before wrapping her in a hug. "Do you want me to come with you?"

Adria shook her head. "No…no…you need to take care of…" She waved her hand around the room at the studio but meant the band, the album, the documentary, and the argument between Landry and Paisley that needed fixing. Normally, Nikki would have been the one to try and bring them back together while Adria forced them into making lists to bang out their differences. It was a skill she'd learned from her father. Negotiation at its best.

Her stomach twisted. *Papá* would have to use those skills now to try and save his youngest child. She'd never lost faith in her father, never in all her twenty-four years, but this…could he do this when there were so many emotions tied to it?

Adria handed Fiadh her phone. "Take this. I can't have it right now. But be careful. If they use it to try and track me…they'll end up with you instead."

Fiadh's eyes were full of concern. "They'll hardly mistake me for you. If it was Landry you were giving your phone to, it would be different."

Adria nodded. It was all she could do.

She grabbed her bag and went to follow the bodyguards from the room, but at the last minute, she turned back with eyes full of unshed tears. Fiadh was at her side once more, hugging her, holding her up. Adria felt the slide of uncharacteristic tears down her cheeks, and it was Fee who leaned away to swipe at them for her.

"She's going to be okay, Adria. They'll find her. But go.

Go so you'll be safe and be able to come back to us soon."

Adria nodded, squeezed Fiadh tightly, and then followed the team out of the room.

The SUVs were dark and tinted just like every set of them they'd been in since the band had taken off, but also like the ones her father had ridden in for decades. Protection from those who targeted him.

As Grand Orchard faded behind them, Adria panicked. What if she couldn't trust these people either? What if they were being paid by the kidnappers? She had no phone. No way of contacting anyone.

She was surrounded by big burly men and one single, equally built woman.

She wasn't alone. And yet every single fiber in her being felt that way.

Her breath came in short pants, her vision turned cloudy, and the woman next to her put a hand on her shoulder, which caused her to jump. The seat belt bit into her skin.

"Breathe," the woman said, and Adria noticed her eyes were kind. Soft and brown like Fiadh's. Like looking through a glass of amber liquid.

Adria nodded.

"Inhale slowly, count to five, hold it for five, and then slowly exhale for another five," the woman instructed.

Adria already knew this. She'd been taught to maintain her control from a young age. Beauty contestants didn't lose their shit unless they wanted to be the first out of the competition. So she did as she was told, repeating the process several times until her shortness of breath eased ever so slightly. Her veins still beat at a wild pace, her heart still pounded as if it was trying to break free, but at least she wasn't going to pass out.

One of the men up front spoke into his earpiece. "We've got Rojas and are twenty minutes out."

The way he said her name in a deep gravelly tone reminded her of Ronan saying any of the nicknames he'd given her in the same way, but with also a taunt to it. A dare.

The only good thing about any of this was that, with both Leya and Adria gone, there was no way Ronan was going to be able to film his documentary tonight. Adria couldn't help the pleasure the thought brought her. He deserved to have his plans screwed up. He'd earned every bit of bad luck being sent his way.

She leaned back against the headrest, turning her eyes to the darkened skies. She watched as the valley turned into hills and the hills turned into mountains outside the window. She said every prayer she could remember learning in her mother's church, hoping, somehow, they would protect her little sister.

Chapter Five

Fiadh

THAT DAY
Performed by Natalie Imbruglia

Fiadh watched as Adria and some of their detail left in a flurry of activity. Her heart pounded out an aching cry for Adria's sister who was bright, beautiful, and fiercely determined to become a pediatrician. A shocked silence filled the studio, and all Fee could think was that everything was crumbling apart.

Landry and Paisley were at each other's throats, Leya was off on the campaign trail, Nikki was hurting, and now Adria was gone…hidden away for who knew how long. This was how bands fell apart. This was how things cracked and fissured.

She couldn't let it happen. She refused to let it happen.

Not when it was all she had left.

She shut that thought down before it could bloom into painful memories of her family. She was happy with her life, spreading love and joy the way she'd always wanted to—through songs—using instruments she'd learned at her mother's feet.

She shook her head again, pushing those thoughts to the background, and turned to their manager. Tommy was dressed like he was a rock star, in black leather and gold chains.

Sometimes, he even acted like one, but he was also very good at what he did. Between him and their label owner, they'd taken The Painted Daisies from obscurity to Grammy-award-winning success in a handful of years.

Lost Heart Records was renowned for finding undiscovered talent and turning them into success stories, but the man who owned it, Nick Jackson, was rarely involved with actually making the music. He preferred the business side of things—copyrights, numbers, and marketing. So, when he'd shown up at the studio today, it had made Fiadh anxious for some reason.

And now, with everything spiraling, she wondered if it had been a sign.

Tommy dragged a hand over his face. "Well, fuck."

The front door of the studio opened, and a man in a suit entered. He was younger than Tommy and Nick, maybe close to thirty, but there was an aura about him that screamed dominance. As if he was the male lion who'd win the battle for the pride even when the other two men had more knowledge and experience. He had dark-brown hair that was shaved slightly on the sides but left longer on the top. There was not a strand out of place, and yet it wasn't gelled into a helmet, like Tommy's. No, it was more like the hair was afraid to move and disappoint its owner. The man's bright-blue eyes took in the handful of people in the room, brows collapsing in on each other and a frown taking his full lips and turning them down. He didn't look like a man who smiled often, and yet the frown also seemed out of place. Like he was better expressionless. Stonelike. Because his chiseled jaw could easily be a sculpture in any museum Fiadh had ever visited.

When he reached them, he took Fee in from head to toe with a careless assessment before he pretty much dismissed her to turn toward Tommy and Nick.

This pissed her off without him ever having opened his mouth.

"Where are the others?" the man asked in lieu of a

greeting.

"Well," Tommy said, dragging his hand over his chin. "We've had some shit hit the fan this afternoon."

Mr. Alpha-Man's jaw ticked, eyes squinting. "What's that supposed to mean?"

"We should postpone this meeting," Nick said. "I've got to get ahold of Ronan Hawk and reschedule the documentary as well."

"Explain," Alpha-Man demanded, and Fiadh bristled, not sure why Nick or Tommy would be taking orders from this unknown asshole.

"Who the hell are you, and why do you think you can come in here and demand anything?" she asked.

Cold eyes landed on her again, his jaw ticking even harder before he settled in on Nick. "You haven't told them?"

Nick straightened his tie and cleared his throat. "I'd planned on it, but as I said, we've had some bumps today. I think it would be best to hold back until we can get everyone together next week."

Alpha-Man glared. "I'm leaving for Germany tomorrow. I'll be there through the end of the month. I have this single window of time, Nick. Unlike these creative types"—his eyes shot to Fiadh again—"I can't just blow where the wind takes me."

What the actual fuck?

"Listen, jer—" Fiadh started, only to be cut off by a woman who emerged from behind Alpha-Man.

"Call your little bandmates, Fiadh. Get them here so Mr. Riggs can talk to them," she said. It wasn't the woman's tone or the fact that she was telling Fee what to do or even her stuck-up attitude that had Fee bristling. Instead, it was because the woman had said her name wrong like a million other assholes had before her. She'd pronounced it, Fee-ah-duh.

A flicker of something like irritation crossed Alpha-

Man's face. He shoved his hands into his pockets and darted a look that could kill at the woman. "It's Fee-uh. Like Thea with an F, Shari."

Fiadh didn't know what to process first. That this man actually knew how to pronounce her name right, that he'd called the woman out on it, or the fact that she'd been commanded to call her friends without Tommy or Nick saying a word.

She turned to the two men the band had trusted for seven years and demanded, "What the hell is going on?"

Nick's eyes lowered to the ground before they raised back up to meet her face, and they were full of unshed tears. Tears that made Fiadh's chest ache and her stomach plummet.

"I've sold the label," he said quietly.

Oh, shit.

Fiadh's legs gave out, and she landed on the arm of a chair behind her.

Nick came over, squatting down in front of her. "My wife's sick, Fee. I just want to spend what's left of her time at her side, giving her the best of everything."

How could she possibly stay angry with him for selling now? For passing them off to someone else when his reason was so noble? So damn good!

"Oh, Nick…I'm so sorry," Fiadh said, putting a hand on his shoulder, true sorrow filling her for him and his family.

Nick stood and waved a hand at Alpha-Man. "This is Asher Riggs. President of Ridgeway Media Industries, which is a conglomerate of paper, TV, and radio media. He's branching out into music, and my label is the second one he's picked up. With all the different avenues his company has at its disposal, it'll increase the options for The Painted Daisies beyond anything I could do for you. You're in good hands."

She doubted it. Nick and Tommy had already made them a worldwide, household name. What more could the suit do for them?

Alpha-Man—Asher—looked down at his watch again and frowned. "The film crew is due at the house in thirty minutes, so why are we talking about postponing?"

Neither Nick nor Tommy jumped in to defend them, so Fee did instead.

"If you must know, Adria's sister was kidnapped, Leya was called to the Democratic Convention, and Nikki's in bed with a migraine," Fiadh said, not daring to mention the squabble going on between Landry and Paisley.

Asher's jaw ticked. "I understand that music takes a bit of…creative license…in order to come to its full potential, but I will never—and I mean never—support us missing commitments. You've signed up to do this documentary with Ronan. The band will fulfill its obligation."

It was said high-handedly, like a father scolding a child, and it made her stiffen even more. Her muscles were wound so tight that if someone touched her, she was sure she'd break apart. She rose, stepped closer to Asher, and twisted her head to glare up at him.

"Listen, jackoff, just because we're artists, doesn't mean we shirk our commitments. We've never jerked anyone around—press, workers, stadiums, or otherwise. Not once. But sometimes, things can't be helped. Like a girl being fecking kidnapped. Or are you hard of hearing and missed that part?"

Her Irish accent coated her nouns and shortened her syllables in a way they hardly did anymore unless she got overly emotional.

Asher's eyes squinted, the blue gaze landing on her and sending icy shivers down her back. Shivers that came with an overpowering awareness of everything about him. The soft hint of an earthy and yet citrusy scent that surrounded him, the way his muscles rippled beneath his suit, and the way those firm, full lips looked entirely too kissable. She despised it— everything about him.

"Adria's absence can easily be explained," he said, tone

sharp and decisive. He shot a look at Nick and Tommy. "I already told you I thought six females in one band is too many. We should cut it down to four. This could be the start."

What the hell? Fiadh stepped closer. "I know I did *not* just hear you suggest we lose two of our members?"

He didn't even blink an eye. "It's more cost-effective without losing the core talent."

"And just who do you think is the core talent? Who the hell do you think we can just drop? Because our drummer happens to be pretty irreplaceable," Fiadh growled, rage and fury flying through her. She knew if she looked in a mirror, her face would be a deep shade of red, and her freckles that normally were hard to see would be popping because of it.

His gaze flickered over her in complete silence.

"Me?" she snarled. "I'm one of the ones to get tossed?" She was going to hit him. She was going to pummel her fists into his massive, muscular chest if she had to stay there. Instead, she pushed passed him and headed for the door, tossing a "Feck you" over her shoulder.

"Fee, that isn't what he meant," Tommy shouted after her.

But it had been. The asshole, new owner of their label had just suggested she be removed from the band. Cut off from her family. The only people who were at her side anymore. Well, screw him. She wasn't going anywhere.

She stomped out to the sidewalk with one of their detail on her heels. She glanced both ways down the street, searching for the dark SUVs that normally waited for them.

The bodyguard behind her said, "I'm sorry, Ms. Kane. The last car took Ms. Rojas into hiding, but Andy, who took Ms. Rani out to the farmhouse, is coming back with the Escalade. We just have to wait a couple of minutes."

Shit. She'd planned her dramatic escape and was now stuck on the curb, twiddling her fingers like some wannabe waiting for the superstar to look her way when *she* was supposed to be the rock star.

The door of the studio opened behind her. Tommy and Asshole-Asher came through, followed by his doting assistant in her tight skirt and Jimmy Choos. Fiadh ignored them all as the bodyguard repeated to Tommy the reason they were waiting.

"We'll take the limo," Asshole-Asher said and stalked on long legs toward one parked around the corner.

"I'm not getting in a car with him, Tommy. Hell will freeze over first," Fiadh said.

Tommy ran a hand through the bristle on his chin. "Play nice, Fee. He can make life miserable for all of us. He owns the label now. He can pull the plug, and you'll be done recording this album altogether. The Painted Daisies will join the host of bands to have come and gone and been forgotten. You want that?"

"He's talking about cutting some of us…cutting me!"

"Asher is just stirring the pot, seeing what falls out. He does it every time he takes over a business. The Painted Daisies are successful because of each of your unique voices, talents, and cultures coming together. He won't carve it up into something less," Tommy insisted.

She wasn't so sure.

Tommy took her by the elbow and pulled her toward the limousine Asher and his little friend had disappeared into.

Fiadh's heart had been heavy before Asher had shown up. Full of worry for her best friend and her sister and the boy who was tearing them apart. Full of concern for Leya trying to fit into the genius family she felt like an ugly duckling in. Aching sorrow for Adria's family struggling with her sister's kidnapping. Fear that Nikki's headaches were more serious than she was letting on. And now…now she felt like all of that was amplified because, while her friends all dealt with these enormous things happening in their lives, the band could be falling apart, and they didn't even know it.

Chapter Six

Jonas

DREAMS

Performed by The Cranberries

Jonas's heart continued to feel shredded as he led Paisley into his apartment. But as he turned from the door to take Paisley in, he couldn't keep the hope from slowly curling through him. There was an unshakeable truth she'd sung about in her lyrics. They fit. They blended together. The jagged pieces of their souls had collided, finding a home. It was as if they'd been two lost scraps drifting in the breeze until the wind had blown them together.

She watched him as he took a step toward her. A tendril of her hair had escaped her clip and fallen in front of her eyes, hiding some of the emotions swimming there. She was completely still, shoulders back, gaze heated, but he also knew she was nervous because her index finger had landed on her birthmark.

"Paisley." Her name came out as an agonized groan, unsure of what was the right thing to do. Push her away or pull her close.

And then, he didn't have a choice because her body collided with his. Her arms went around his neck, and she stood on her tiptoes to join their mouths together just like she had on the sidewalk. Heat traveled through him, curls of desire leaving a heady trail as it worked its way through every vein and nerve ending until his body was standing at attention, ready to surrender after the frenzied battle with passion and restraint he'd been waging for days.

He put his arms around her waist, lifted her with ease, and set her on the counter in the bite-sized kitchen. Standing between her legs, he trailed his fingers and mouth down her face, her neck, and her chest. He swooped aside the tank top she wore that barely hid the pink Sweet Memory daisy tattooed there and lavished a taut nipple with his tongue. Paisley moaned, arching into him, hands mussing with his hair before she reached for his T-shirt and tugged.

He stepped back, lifting his shirt from the back, pulling it off, and tossing it aside. Then, he lifted her tank and did the same, unhooking her bra before sliding their bodies back together and relishing in the perfect warmth of their skin gliding together.

Their mouths fused hungrily, tongues seeking their inner recesses while fingers explored. The air grew heavier, thicker, fuller. She moaned and the sound had him straining against his jeans, the pressure almost unbearable.

"Take me to your bed, Jonas," Paisley demanded, her voice deeper than he'd ever heard it before. More like her sister's than her own soft one.

He rested his forehead on her chest, eyes closed, listening to the rhythm of her heartbeat.

"No," he said quietly.

She drew his chin up, searching his face with eyes that ached. "Why?"

He couldn't voice all his reasons for stopping them. Fear of losing her. Fear of doing something she'd hate him for. Fear that her friends and sister would hate him even more. Fear that was ridiculous. He didn't know one heterosexual man his age who would have said no to Paisley's demand. They would have simply fucked her senseless. And maybe that was yet another of the many reasons he wouldn't. He refused to be just some damn guy who screwed her until she screamed.

Not that he was sure he could even make her scream. He wasn't sure he could even last long enough to give her the climax she deserved. But that wasn't the point, and he couldn't voice any of those fears, so he said the one thing that was closest to the surface. "I'm not going to make love to you just so you can spite Landry."

He regretted it as soon as he said it.

She inhaled sharply, pain hitting her eyes, and then she was pushing him away. She jumped off the counter, retrieved her clothes, and reassembled them on her body all while he watched.

When she lifted her beautiful eyes to his face, they were no longer soft. They were hard and angry, but she was still painfully quiet when she finally spoke.

"You really think I'd do that to either of us?" she demanded, hands on her hips, looking very much like some fiery sprite. "Bring her anger into this with us?"

He ran a hand through his hair, wondering how he was going to get out of this without pissing her off or leaving more wounds on her heart.

"I think, right now, you want to prove she's wrong."

Her eyes closed and opened almost as if the words had been a slap to her face. "She is. But that isn't why I want this. I want this because I never feel like I'm truly home until you're touching me. I want to know what it feels like when you're fully inside me and our bodies become one. I want to find the end of the song we've written together. There's no reason to keep stopping us."

He swallowed hard, her words echoing what he'd been thinking moments before and settling into his heart like a Band-Aid over cracks that always seemed to bleed. But he reminded himself of the harshest truth. The number one reason he refused her. He simply wasn't sure he was the man she deserved. Not yet. Maybe never. Right now, he was still a broken kid who tended to ruin everything he touched with roiling anger.

He had so much work to do before he became…something worthy. He wasn't sure he'd ever get there, but he wanted to try because Paisley Kim…she was his whole world. A shiny star in a sea of dark. She brought so much damn beauty into his life that it physically hurt, and he wanted to make sure he could give her the same thing back.

Paisley closed the distance between them, drawing his hand into hers, aligning their palms.

"Two years, Jonas. I've missed you…wanted this…for two years. And now that we're here, this close, I don't want her to be the reason we aren't together." Paisley shook her head, tears filling her eyes.

Jonas swallowed. "We barely knew each other then, sweetheart. And now…now I've got a lot of things to work on, and I think you know that as much as Landry does."

"We belong together. We're two pieces of a whole. You need me to ground you, and I need you to lift me up," Paisley said quietly, eyes begging him to admit the truth. "She shouldn't be able to take that from us."

He nodded. Unable to see the pain in her eyes without touching her, he pulled her close and held on tight. "She won't. But you have to remember, she loves you too. She loved you first, and no matter what I said back there, she does want what's best for you."

"Only if it's what's best for her as well," Paisley said, and it sounded sad and tired, as if she couldn't fight the world one more second.

"I don't think you really believe that."

They were silent for a long moment, and Jonas tugged her toward the couch. When he got there, he pulled her onto his lap, and she rested her head on his chest. They sat that way for a long time, just listening to each other's heartbeats as the sun slanted across the sky and the room grew dim.

After what felt like days, she finally broke the quiet, asking, "Do you remember the very first argument we had about ABBA?"

He laughed softly. "I still think they're shit, but if Brady's daughter heard me say that, she'd skewer me alive."

"Normally, when someone challenges me, I can't breathe. I can't talk. I freeze. It's like I'm a deer caught in the headlights. But with you…all the thoughts inside of me pour out easily. Freely. That first time we argued, you just stared at me as if my words were awe-inspiring, revolutionary. It was like you could actually see me. The real me. The one who's afraid to be onstage and has anxiety attacks, and sometimes can't even speak when someone asks her a question."

Jonas hated her anxiety almost as much as he hated the way she doubted her opinions were valid. She had so much to say, so much talent to share, and yet she'd always hidden it behind Landry because she'd been afraid to step out of the shadows. She deserved more than the sliver of light the band shined her way. Landry was pissed that Paisley was starting to see that. It challenged the status quo. And when that happened, there were always arguments. Adjustments. He had to believe they'd get through it though, because they loved each other.

Pounding on the door caused Jonas's eyes to fly in that direction, cutting him off from saying anything more. He dragged himself up, threw on his T-shirt, and opened it.

Trevor stood there, frowning.

"Hey," Jonas said, his brow furrowing as concern flew through him.

"Dylan went back with Landry, so I grabbed a car to take you to the farmhouse for the bonfire," Trevor said.

Jonas looked back at Paisley waiting on the couch. "We gotta go, Paise."

She flicked her eyes to the darkened windows and jumped up. "Crud. How late is it?"

"You still have time," Trevor answered.

"But Landry needed help setting up," she said, regret filling her tone because even still angry and upset with her sister, she hated letting Landry down.

Jonas followed Paisley as she all but ran down the steps after Trevor. Once they were loaded into the SUV and headed out of town, Paisley ran a hand through her long hair, as if trying to straighten it, before pushing into her birthmark with her fingertip. He could almost feel the nervousness crawling through her veins as if it was its own entity. This was more than just concern about Landry. She was worried because she was supposed to talk with Ronan again tonight, and she hadn't decided whether to tell him about her anxiety and stage fright or not.

Paisley's phone started to blow up just as Trevor's did the same thing in the front. Ping after ping.

"What is it?" Jonas asked.

"Oh my God," Paisley said, color draining from her face as she flicked through the messages.

He pulled her close, pulse quickening. "What's wrong?"

"Adria's sister was kidnapped!"

Jonas's eyes met Trevor's in the rearview mirror, dread curling through him.

"Her dad received a ransom note, and the detail has taken Adria to some undisclosed location because he's worried that whoever did this will come for her too."

Goosebumps littered his skin as Paisley turned to him with panic written on her face and her hands trembling.

"Leya's gone to D.C. early for the convention, and Fiadh has something to tell us about Nick's label." Her eyes filled with tears. "What on earth happened after we left this afternoon?"

Jonas's stomach spasmed. In a ridiculous series of blows the band was teetering and Paisley right along with it. He struggled to quell his nerves, to find a sense of calm so he could be the stable ground beneath her feet. He tugged her into his chest and wrapped his arms around her.

When they pulled up in front of the farmhouse, there was a van there. Ronan had brought in a film crew for the bonfire, and they were unloading equipment in the near darkness with only the porchlight illuminating the drive. He lifted his chin in their direction as Paisley and Jonas slid out of the back of the SUV.

Ronan sauntered over to them with an unnecessary beanie covering his hair. Jonas's stomach tightened, hating his arrogant assuredness. Hating that this man would have no qualms asking Paisley questions that would upset her even more—all for the sake of his damn film.

"Hey, no one answered when I knocked. Wasn't sure what was up. I kind of expected everyone to be here primping," Ronan said, gray eyes twinkling and lips twitching as if he'd said something hilarious.

"Only Landry and Nikki are here at the moment," Paisley said, finger pushing into her star. "There's a lot going on."

Ronan frowned, waiting for her to explain, but she didn't. She turned and ran for the front door instead.

"We'll just head over to the pond and get things set up," Ronan called after her, his brows bent in confusion.

Jonas jogged after Paisley, and if he hadn't been right behind her, he wouldn't have seen her stiffen or seen the shiver that went through her.

"What?" he asked, and when she didn't move, when she continued to stare at the door as if it was a ghost, he moved around to see what had caused her to go numb.

There was a picture taped well below the handle, as if someone had been ducking out of the camera's view while sticking it there. It was of Jonas and Paisley from that afternoon as they'd left the studio and locked lips in the middle of the street. The image had words scrawled on top of it. Words that were running in deep red and turned Jonas's stomach.

You'll die before I let you be happy.

The red dripped into the two deep grooves carved into Jonas's and Paisley's faces.

Emotions swam through him so fast it was hard to capture them. Fear. Panic. Anger. Disgust. And then back to fear. Regardless of everything else going on with the band tonight, this…this seemed to be about them.

Chapter Seven

Landry

SOUND OF SILENCE
Performed by Disturbed

The air was still heavy even as the sun sank below the treetops. The humidity of upstate New York in summer wasn't anything to joke about. But then, lately, Landry couldn't find much of anything to joke about. There were days when she felt like she was the only one even trying to keep the band moving forward. Like if she wasn't there, it would all collapse. It was a heavy burden.

Landry pushed aside the brush as she made her way around the barely visible trail surrounding Swan River Pond. It was her favorite thing about the farmhouse. The water…the swans…the escape it allowed her from the others while she attempted to assemble her thoughts into some kind of order.

She was almost silent as she jogged along the grassy path in her bright-yellow sneakers and neon workout gear. Her long hair kept flying in her face. She swiped at it, frustrated she'd forgotten a hairband in her hurry to get out the door and back before she had to set up for Ronan and his crew. She probably should have skipped the jog tonight—another mistake she'd made in a long line of them lately.

Landry rounded the last corner of the pond, bringing the farmhouse into view. She stopped at the shoreline, turning away from the handful of lights that glittered from the windows, to try and catch her breath before she went in. The pond was swathed in shadow, making it almost impossible to see much past the beam of her phone's flashlight. Even with a member of their detail following several yards behind her, it had been stupid to go running this late. If Paisley had done it, she would have read her the riot act.

Just thinking of Paisley made her chest ache more than it had from the run.

That had been Landry's biggest screw-up yet. The things she'd said to Paisley and Jonas were almost unforgivable. She wasn't sure if her little sister would accept her apology, even if she found the courage to give her the note she'd written. Landry closed her eyes as she faced the pond, wishing for a breeze that wasn't there and trying to hold back the tears. For two years, she'd watched as Paisley built a friendship with Jonas over texts and long-distance chats, and for two years, she'd done her best to minimize their relationship to her sister.

It wasn't just that they'd been young when they first met—Landry would be hypocritical if she'd said that was it when she'd had a slew of people in and out of her life well before she'd hit her twenties. It was more of what she'd told her friends. She didn't want Paisley's romanticism and loyalty to tie her to the first person who came along—a boy she rarely saw and who had a troubled past that screamed from his tortured eyes. A guy who was the reason they were receiving ugly notes with their faces scratched out.

You know that's not the real reason, her conscience yelled at her.

Okay, so the truth was she'd also been afraid of losing her sister. Afraid of no longer being the one person Paisley relied on to hold her up when she was falling. Of not being the one who believed in Paisley more than anyone else. Because her little sister was absolutely and undeniably the most talented one of them all. Her voice was the strongest, and her words were the reason they had anything to sing to begin with.

Without Paisley, The Painted Daisies wouldn't exist.

Or they'd exist, but they'd be just another "girl band" who'd come and gone because they were singing words someone else had created. For the first year after she and Fiadh had formed the band in high school, they'd sung cover songs while playing whatever gig they could get. It wasn't until Landry had forced Paisley to share her songs with the others that they'd really taken off. It was Paisley's voice and words that had first drawn Nick Jackson's attention.

The fear Landry had felt two years ago, watching as Paisley and Jonas built a tentative friendship, was nothing to what she felt now. The rift between them felt like a huge canyon she wasn't sure how to navigate before the band crumbled apart.

She swallowed hard. Truth was, she was even more afraid of the tension between them than she was of the stupid notes warning that hell was going to rain down on them. Or maybe she was afraid that what she'd told Ronan she wanted for Paisley was actually happening. That Paisley was coming out of the shadows to take the lead, and it would leave Landry with nothing.

While Landry was confident their security team and the police would find whoever this was coming for them, there was no one to handle the gaping hole Landry herself had caused.

A tear slowly traveled down her cheek, and she brushed it away.

A noise drew her head in Ramona's direction. Her bodyguard had followed her around the lake at a respectful distance, giving Landry her space. She felt slightly guilty that she'd forced the woman out in the heat and the darkness. Landry used her phone light to shine back toward the path, surprised when she didn't see the bodyguard.

She shrugged it off, assuming it was one of the swans or other waterfowl that made the pond their home, but then the hair on the back of her neck rose. A warning that came too late. She started to call out to Ramona as a black-gloved hand slid over her mouth from behind, and a muscled body slammed her back against it.

Shock hit her first. Panic second.

She struggled, trying to bite the hand covering her mouth, trying to slam her foot into a knee or drag it down a shin.

A new terror hammered through her as the truth hit home. She couldn't escape. He was too strong, too well trained, easily countering her weak moves. Where was the rest of her security? Where were her friends? Her sister? The people who should have been flowing into the backyard for Ronan's documentary?

Doors slammed in the distance, and through the fear, relief and hope tried to filter in as she heard Ronan's deep voice giving directions to his crew.

She just had to get free enough to scream.

As if he'd read her thoughts, the arms around her tightened, squeezing until the air left her gut in a single whoosh. A knife flashed before her eyes, glinting in the ghostly white light of her phone that had fallen to the ground.

The slow tears that had come when she'd been thinking of Paisley were replaced with a rush of them. Fast and furious. She didn't want to die. She had too much still to do. Too many things to beg forgiveness for.

But it was too late. The knife was there. The pain was sharp and fierce as the edge bit into her neck and...

Chapter Eight

Paisley

GONE AWAY
Performed by The Offspring

The blood dripping from the image of Jonas and her made her stomach lurch.

Whoever was doing this had been there on the street today. Watching them. Filming them. Why hadn't their security seen them? Why was this happening at all?

Landry!

Paisley grabbed the handle above the picture and thrust open the door. "Landry! Nikki!" she called into the quiet of the house.

There were a few lights on, a lamp in the downstairs living room and the can lights in the kitchen, but other than that, the house was still and shadowy.

"Landry!" Paisley cried again, scrambling for the stairs with Jonas and Trevor right behind her. She threw open the door of her sister's room with her pulse hammering. It was empty, but the outfit she'd had on earlier was tossed on the bed, which meant she'd been there.

Knowing Landry, she'd gone for a run around the pond. It was late and dark, but that hadn't stopped her the other night. Paisley turned to leave and saw Trevor throwing open other doors, calling for Landry and Nikki.

She heard Nikki's voice, groggy and startled. Paisley raced down the hall just as Nikki sat up in bed wearing nothing but a camisole and underwear. There was a glazed expression on her face that she often had when fighting her migraines.

"Have you seen Landry?" Trevor demanded.

Nikki shook her head, wincing.

They all ran down the stairs, searching the other rooms.

Later, Paisley would doubt what had sent her out the back door. It was as if she heard Landry calling her but from far away, like through a crowd that was loud and clamoring.

She flipped on the porch lights, stepped out onto the wooden slats, and rushed to the edge, searching the darkness. There. Down by the pond, a soft light like a phone glowed. Thank God.

"Landry!" Paisley called in relief.

She flew down the stairs and out toward the water. As Paisley drew closer, fear drifted back in. The phone was on the ground, and a dark mound lay beside it.

"Landry…" Paisley called softly this time as her skin broke out in goosebumps, even though the night was hot and humid.

"Lan," Paisley called.

She was near enough now to know it was actually Landry on the ground. The bright-yellow sneakers she'd had made to match the Golden Butterfly daisy the world associated with her were glowing in the darkness. But Landry wasn't moving. She just lay there.

Paisley's vision blurred, ice filled her veins, and she had to force herself past it in order reach down and touch Landry's shoulder. "Lan…"

Her sister sagged, and that's when Paisley saw it. The blood. The gaping wound at Landry's neck. The unfocused, staring eyes. She screamed. She screamed Landry's name. She screamed at the horror. She screamed and screamed and screamed.

Strong arms wrapped around her waist, and she fought against them before Jonas's deep voice spoke near her ear, "I got you, Paise. I got you."

Trevor appeared, stepping around them and grabbing Landry's wrist, checking for a pulse before blocking Paisley's view of her sister. But even with Trevor's muscled torso in front of her, all she could see was Landry's face and the dark, gruesome cut on her neck.

Paisley's voice was hoarse. Was she still screaming? The screams turned into violent sobs as she pushed her face into Jonas's chest.

"God, Paise. Jesus... Trevor, what the hell?" Jonas's voice broke with raw emotions.

Trevor put his arms around them both, hugging them tightly as if he could somehow take away what they'd seen. Make it better. Fix it. Fix her sister.

She dragged herself away from them both, somehow fighting off their muscled arms. She fell to the ground, hands pushed to her stomach as she knelt at her sister's side. "Landry... Don't leave, Landry. I'm sorry. I'm so sorry. I love you. I love you! Do you hear me? God. Please don't die."

Chapter Nine

Jonas

EVERYBODY HURTS
Performed by The Corrs

Jonas's chest was on fire, agony ripping through him at Paisley's pained cries. Her tortured words. He wrapped his arms around her, lifting her from where she'd collapsed next to her sister.

Paisley kicked out. "Let me go."

"Paise, come away. You can't. You don't want to see this. Come away." His voice was crammed with tears. For her. For Landry. For all of them.

"Make her live, Trevor! Make her live. Get the ambulance. The doctors. Make her live!" she screamed at Trevor standing in front of her sister's body, blocking them from the gruesome sight. But it was too late. It was burned into his irises.

Jonas carried Paisley away, taking her back toward the house.

At the top of the porch steps, Nikki waited, hand to her mouth, horror in her eyes.

"No… No!" Nikki said, shaking her head, fear and sorrow echoed in her words. It made Paisley's tight body crumple into violent sobs in his arms.

Jonas grabbed Nikki's hand, pulling her into the house

with them.

He set Paisley down on the couch in the front room, and Nikki collapsed next to her, hugging Paisley to her chest like Jonas wanted to do.

Ronan stood there with his crew behind him, cameras rolling, as sirens ripped through in the air.

"What is it?" Ronan asked, looking at Jonas with the most serious expression on his face he'd ever seen on the man.

Jonas shook his head. He had no words to describe what he'd seen, especially not on camera.

"Turn the fucking cameras off," Jonas said.

Ronan bristled. "We're here—"

Jonas reached over to the man holding the camera next to Ronan and placed a hand over the lens. "Turn the fucking cameras off before I toss them all in the pond."

Jonas's voice was laced with both threats and promises. Ones he would absolutely follow through on just as he had with Larry the day before. The cameraman looked to Ronan, and Ronan nodded. The camera light went out, and Jonas turned back to Paisley and Nikki.

He fell at Paisley's feet, grabbed her hand, and put it on his cheek. "Paisley. I got you. I'm here."

Paisley's eyes lifted from Nikki's chest. They were red-rimmed and tortured. Her voice almost disappeared as she whispered the words, "That picture on the door… Is this our fault? Did that happen… Did he think she was me?"

Jonas's heart clogged his throat, making it hard to breathe. He didn't know what to say. He didn't know the right answer. Thoughts of the blood dripping from the photograph and the image of Landry's neck sliced open caused his stomach to lurch, threatening to let loose everything he'd eaten at lunch.

The house filled with police and the Daisies' security team. Marco strode through the room as if he owned it, the other security detail making room for their leader. His face was impassive until he saw Jonas, and then relief filled it, dark eyes meeting his. "Thank God, you're okay."

But his words caused Paisley to convulse, and a wounded cry ripped from her because her sister wasn't okay. Her sister was dead.

Marco looked regretful, rubbed a hand through his hair, and then tilted his head at Jonas toward the kitchen.

Jonas looked at Paisley and Nikki huddled on the couch, tears pouring down their faces. "I'll be right back, Paisley. I'll be right in the kitchen."

He didn't know what else to say. He didn't know how else to help, except to let her know he was there. That he wasn't going anywhere.

When they got to the kitchen, Marco wrapped Jonas in a hug that was tight and hard, as if he was afraid to let him go, and Jonas hugged him back equally as hard. He needed his brother's strength to wash off on him so he could be strong for Paisley.

"Jo-Jo," Marco said.

"Where the fuck was her security?" Jonas said into his shoulder.

"Ramona's dead too," Marco said quietly. "Trevor found her."

Fuck.

"I'm going out there to help with the investigation. You going to be okay in here?" Marco asked.

Jonas nodded even though he wasn't sure it was true.

Marco squeezed him one more time and then left out the back. Jonas turned around, heading for Paisley, as the front door burst open, and Fiadh rushed in. Tommy and Nick were at her side with some man in a suit Jonas had never seen before.

Fiadh's wide eyes met Jonas's.

"Tell me…just…" Her voice trailed off as she saw Paisley

and Nikki wrapped together, weeping.

Fiadh's throat bobbed as she whispered, "Lan…"

Jonas swallowed hard, and the words came out like a croak. "She's…she's dead."

Tears filled Fiadh's eyes, and then they were pouring down her face as she joined the other two women on the couch, locking them in a fierce embrace.

"Fuck," the man in the suit said, flicking his hand over his jacket as if brushing off lint. He looked at Nick and said with a blandness that seemed completely out of place, given the situation, "I guess that discount I asked for is going to be back on the table."

Nick blanched but ignored the man. Instead, he turned to Ronan and the crew. "I think it's best if you leave."

"We don't want anyone going anywhere," a police officer said from behind them. "Everyone who was on the property needs to stay put until we have a chance to debrief them."

In the officer's hand was the picture that had been on the door—the picture of Paisley and Jonas with their faces scratched out in blood.

Despair sliced its way through Jonas's heart. Was Paisley right? Had Landry been killed because of them?

Chapter Ten

I WILL NOT SAY GOODBYE

Performed by Danny Gokey

NIKKI

They came and tore the property apart. FBI. Police. Garner Security.

But none of it could change the fact that Landry was dead.

Paisley and Jonas thought it was because of them.

The officials weren't so sure. According to them, the creepy stalker notes were erratic and amateurish, whereas at first glance, Landry had been killed by someone trained to do so.

An officer approached Nikki, said the Professor was there to see her, and asked if she wanted him to send the man away. Nikki turned a wide-eyed gaze toward the open front door and the sea of officials who'd been pouring in and around the property. She'd forgotten about him. Forgotten about the torn-up office and the rough man who'd been with him. She didn't know if she wanted to see him. Not now. Not after what had happened.

Maynard looked wild-eyed, and she was afraid he wouldn't leave, so she pulled herself from the couch and joined him on the porch. He whispered in her ear, dark thoughts. He said this could have been *THEM* coming for her like they'd come for him earlier in the day just for trying to find the truth.

Landry and Nikki were almost identical from the back when she had her hair straightened. Same height. Same body shape.

Her stomach turned.

Could this have been because of her? Her family? The secrets the professor hinted at?

"My brother was right. We need to drop the entire thing. If you say anything, if you try to find out the truth, you risk not only your life but your mother's and the rest of the band's. You don't know who you can trust. They came for your father, they'll come for you and kill whoever is in their path," he whispered. At his office, he'd been afraid but still eager, almost desperate. Now, there was only pure terror in his voice.

A horrified tremor went through her.

She believed him with a sickening clarity. Because Landry was dead. She was dead even though they'd had a host of bodyguards and law enforcement agencies watching over them.

"I'm done, but this," he shoved a small package at her, "it belongs to you. Take it. Don't show it to anyone. Ever."

Nikki tried to push it away, but he pried her fingers open and placed it her palm.

"Good luck, Ms. Rani. I hope you stay safe," he said stepping back.

She would have protested. She would have thrown the package at him if two people hadn't emerged behind him in the darkness. One tall and somber in a dress with her brown hair pulled back into a bun and the other tall and wide-shouldered with a frame that screamed military. Sadness and relief flew through her as she rushed down the steps.

"Mom!" Nikki cried, throwing herself into her mom's strong arms. Her stepmom squeezed her back.

"What's happened?" her father's best friend asked.

Bile rose in her throat. She'd happened. Her curiosity. Her desire to know more about a family she'd never know because her father was no longer alive to answer the questions. The loss of Lan could be her fault.

She promised herself right then that she'd forget it all. That she would never again risk her friends…her mom…herself… to chase a fairytale.

Her mind flashed back to the muscled and tattooed man she'd seen outside the studio and Maynard's scarred brother with his beady eyes.

She hadn't said anything about either of them to her team.

She should have said something.

But now it was too late.

Now she could only bite her tongue and hope the swells of guilt and sorrow didn't drown her.

♫ ♫ ♫

FIADH

She hugged her friends, her bandmates, her sisters fiercely and tightly to her. She'd thought it was all falling apart, and it was, but not in the way she'd expected.

Fee listened while Asher Riggs calmly talked to their label owner about money, and discounts, and a band that would no longer be the flagship of the label, and her stomach twisted and turned.

He'd wanted to get rid of some of them.

He'd wanted four instead of six.

And now there were only five.

She shook her head. It was a ridiculous thought. He wouldn't have had to kill one of them to do it. He'd just fire them. Tear them apart that way.

But when Asher took a call and spoke quietly into the phone, saying, "It's done," all the hair on the back of her neck stood on end.

When he looked up, he caught her gaze, and she sent daggers into him, burning him with an intensity that had him frowning.

If he was behind this, she'd make it her mission to destroy him bit by tiny bit.

♫ ♫ ♫

LEYA

Her hand shook so hard the phone fell from her grasp, and her knees gave out.

Special Agent Kent caught her, picking up the phone and listening to the voice on the other end repeating what they'd told her.

Pain lodged somewhere in her stomach, dragging through her as he set her down on a couch in the living room of the hotel suite.

Had this been what it felt like? The knife slicing through Landry's throat?

"What is it?" her mother asked, rushing over to them.

"She's dead…she's dead…someone killed her," Leya tried to say, but it came out as a garbled collection of words that made no sense.

It was the broody agent who explained it to her mother.

Her mother was not a woman who was afraid. She cut brains open with a steady hand regularly, and yet Leya saw the fear that crossed over her features.

They stepped away as her mother's voice dropped so she wouldn't hear. Except, she did because her brain was hypersensitive, trying to process everything, trying to not feel the agony.

"You don't think…the white supremacists that have been coming after…" her mother's voice faded away. "They all look so alike…"

Holden Kent sent a look in Leya's direction. He hesitated, but then he shook his head.

"I don't think so."

"Think?! *Think* isn't good enough, Special Agent Kent. Find out. Find out for sure."

He nodded and left the room.

Her mother returned to her, wrapping her tight against her chest with the scent of Chanel drifting over them. It didn't provide Leya the comfort it normally did. Instead, the pain in her grew until it felt like it would become the only thing she knew.

Was Landry dead because they'd thought it was Leya on the shore? A warning to her father to give up his nomination as vice president?

♫ ♫ ♫

ADRIA

Lana was the female bodyguard who'd taken Adria from Grand Orchard to the cabin in the middle of nowhere. The bodyguard's phone rang not long after they'd settled in. Hope and fear cut through Adria. She needed them to find her sister whole and well. Lana's eyes cut directly to her. The bodyguard's cheek ticked, her jaw tightened, and Adria could read the truth.

It wasn't good news.

Tears welled in Adria's eyes before Lana even opened her mouth.

"It's not your sister. We're still waiting to hear from your father. This. This is about your band. About Landry."

Adria stared at her, not quite comprehending even as she spoke, the words blending into nonsense. Something about Landry and her throat and the fact that she was no longer with them.

Adria shook her head. No. No, it couldn't be.

"You're wrong," Adria hissed.

Lana looked sad, shaken.

It hit Adria.

The men who'd taken her sister. They'd been coming for her as well.

Her gut heaved, anger and fear and guilt scoring their way through the pain.

Was this because of her?

Because of her family?

The four of them looked so much alike from behind. It would be especially hard to tell them apart in the dark.

It could have been Adria standing by the pond.

Landry could be dead because of her family.

Chapter Eleven

Paisley

SLIPPED AWAY
Performed by Avril Lavigne

Instead of rejoining her family and friends, Paisley did what she'd been doing every day since coming home. She retreated to her sister's room, grabbed Landry's guitar, and clambered onto the yellow-and-orange floral cushion in the window seat that looked over the backyard. Jonas wasn't on the swings anymore. Her heart flipped, and her stomach sagged. He'd left. Just like she'd told him to.

She leaned her head against the paned glass, the coolness calming her somehow. Just like Landry had always calmed her. When her anxiety spiked the worst, it was Landry who'd always saved her. She'd tug at Paisley's hair, surround her hands with her own, and push her metal rings into Paisley's skin. The rings they'd buried her with today.

The pressure grew inside her chest and throat, swelling, swelling, swelling. She rubbed a finger over the new anxiety ring her doctor had prescribed, fighting the tide, trying to push it all back down. The beads on the ring slid back and forth, somehow soothing her and reminding her of Landry all at the same time.

"Your funeral was today," Paisley said, talking to Landry as she'd been doing in secret for days. "It was unbearable, and every time I tried to grab your hand to help me through it, I was torn apart all over again because it was you we were burying."

The silence of the room echoed back.

Not even a ghost of her sister remained. She'd heard one tormented call that night in Grand Orchard—a voice that had said her name in the dark before it had vanished. She'd heard nothing since then, but she could hope. She plucked a chord on the guitar, wishing the sound was Landry's voice answering.

"Jonas has been trying, Lan. He's tried so hard to be there, to stand beside me. And all I can think is that if I hadn't been off with him… If I hadn't been so determined to prove you wrong, to cast you off, to shine on my own, I would've been at your side. You wouldn't have died. That asshole would have found me instead of you."

The well broke over, a sob erupting from deep within her.

"You got what you wanted, Lan. Jonas and I are not together anymore. I can't look at him without seeing all my mistakes. Somehow, I know this wouldn't make you happy. You wouldn't want to tear *me* apart just to tear *us* apart. But it's happened anyway."

Paisley fingered the strings more and then slid her hand down to the Golden Butterfly daisy etched and painted into the rich wood as tears tumbled from her face onto the smooth surface. The more Paisley tried to brush them away, the stronger they came, her loss of Landry mingling with her loss of Jonas.

She tried to force the pain back, turning her thoughts from the two people who'd meant everything and were now gone. Forcing herself to think of the band and Tommy's words.

"Asher and RMI won't wait, Lan. He only cares about money, but the rest of us…we don't know how to do this without you. You'd be making a list, and placing calls, and pushing us all back together, but none of us know how to be you. Not even Fee…"

Another violent sob erupted from her chest. Paisley plucked the strings again. She could play the guitar, but it wasn't her favorite. The piano was where her soul really belonged. Except, these days, the words and the notes that were always rattling around in her brain were quiet—silent—as if even the music was mourning.

"I don't know if we can be The Painted Daisies without you." She sniffled. "I miss you. I wish I knew what to do. I wish…"

Paisley looked down at the guitar case and saw a piece of paper tucked into the inside back pocket. It must have come loose after all the times Paisley had batted the case around over the last few days. She grabbed it, opened it, and read…

♫ ♫ ♫

Need to know who murdered Landry? Or maybe you want to see how each of The Painted Daisies face murder and betrayal while finding love?

<u>The complete series is available now on Amazon!</u>

QR Code:
The Painted Daisies
on Amazon

Want to hear the song, "The Legacy," that Paisley writes for Landry after reading the letter? Listen to it now brought to life by Aly Stiles:

https://geni.us/TheLegacy

Get the entire series today:

Sweet Memory — Paisley & Jonas

An opposite-side-of-the-tracks, second-chance romance

The world's sweetest rock star falls for a troubled music producer whose past comes back to haunt them.

Green Jewel — Fiadh & Asher

An enemies-to-lovers, single-dad romance

He did it. She'll prove it. Her body's reaction to him be damned.

Cherry Brandy — Leya & Holden

A forced-proximity, bodyguard romance

Being on the run with only one bed is no excuse to touch her…until touching is the only choice.

Blue Marguerite — Adria & Ronan

A celebrity, second-chance, frenemy romance

She vowed to never forgive him...not even when he offers answers her family desperately seeks.

Royal Haze — Nikki & D'Angelo

A bodyguard, on-the-run romance with a morally gray hero

He was ready to torture, steal, and kill to defend the world he believed in. What he wasn't prepared for…was her.

About the Author

Award winning author, LJ Evans, lives in Northern California with her husband, child, and the three terrors called cats. She's been writing, almost as a compulsion, since she was a little girl and will often pull the car over to write when a song lyric strikes her. A former first-grade teacher, she now spends her free time reading and writing, as well as binge-watching original shows like *Wednesday, The Mentalist, Veronica Mars,* and *Stranger Things.*

If you ask her the one thing she won't do, it's pretty much anything that involves dirt—sports, gardening, or otherwise. But she loves to write about all of those things, and her first published heroine was pretty much involved with dirt on a daily basis, which is exactly why LJ loves fiction novels—the characters can be everything you're not and still make their way into your heart.

Her novel, **CHARMING AND THE CHERRY BLOSSOM**, was *Writer's Digest* Self-Published E-book Romance of the Year in 2021. For more information about LJ, check out any of these sites:

www.ljevansbooks.com

FaceBook Group: LJ's Music & Stories
LJ Evans on Amazon, Bookbub, and Goodreads
@ljevansbooks on Facebook, Instagram, TikTok, and Pinterest

Books by L J

Standalone

After All the Wreckage— Rory & Gage

A single-dad, small-town, romantic suspense

He's a broody bar owner raising his siblings. She's a scrappy PI who's loved him since she was a teenager. When his brother disappears, she forces aside years of pining and family secrets to help him.

Charming and the Cherry Blossom — Elle & Hudson

A contemporary romance with hints of magical realism

Today was a fairy tale…I inherited a fortune from a dad I never knew, and a thoroughly charming guy asked me out. But like all fairy tales, mine has a dark side...and my happily ever after may disappear with the truth.

The Hatley Family Standalones

The Last One You Loved — Maddox & McKenna

A single-dad, small-town romance

He's a small-town sheriff with a secret that can unravel their worlds. She's an ER resident running from a costly mistake. Coming home will only mean heartache…unless they let forgiveness heal them both.

The Last Promise You Made — Ryder & Gia

A single-dad, small-town, romantic suspense

He's a grumpy rancher who swore off all relationships. She's a spitfire undercover agent who brings danger to his life. Not even a common enemy can force them to trust each other. Desire is an inconvenience. Falling in love is absolutely out of the question.

Perfectly Fine — Gemma & Rex

A fish-out-of-water, celebrity romance

He's a charming, A-list actor at the top of his game. She's a determined, small-town screenwriter hoping for a deal. They form an unexpected connection until heartbreak ruins their future. Available on Amazon and also FREE with newsletter subscription.

My Life as an Album Series

My Life as a Country Album — Cam's Story

A boy-next-door, small-town romance

This is tomboy Cam's diary-style, coming-of-age story about growing up loving the football hero next door. She vowed to love him forever. But when fate comes calling, will she ever find a heart to call home? Warning: Tears may fall.

My Life as a Pop Album — Mia & Derek

A rock star, road-trip romance

Bookworm Mia is trying to put years of guilt behind her when soulful musician Derek Waters strolls into her life and turns it upside down. Once he's seen her, Derek can't walk away unless Mia comes with him. But what will happen when their short time together comes to an end?

My Life as a Rock Album — Seth & PJ

A second-chance, antihero romance

Recovering addict Seth Carmen is a trash artist who knows he's better off alone. But when he finds and loses the love of his life, he can't help sending her a host of love letters to try to win her back. Can Seth prove to PJ they can make broken beautiful?

My Life as a Mixtape — Lonnie & Wynn

A single-dad, rock star romance

Lonnie's always seen relationships as a burden instead of a gift, and picking up the pieces his sister leaves behind is just one of the reasons. When Wynn enters his life just as her world is disintegrating, their mixed-up pasts give way to new beginnings neither of them saw coming.

My Life as a Holiday Album – 2nd Generation

A small-town romance

Come home for the holidays with this heartwarming, full-length standalone full of hidden secrets, true love, and the real meaning of family. Perfect for lovers of *Love Actually* and Hallmark movies, this sexy story intertwines the lives of six couples as they find their way to their happily ever afters with the help of family and friends.

My Life as an Album Series Box Set

The 1st four Album series stories plus an exclusive novella

In the exclusive novella, *This Life with Cam*, Blake Abbott writes to Cam about just what it was like to grow up in the shadow of her relationship with Jake and just when he first fell for the little girl with the popsicle-stained lips. Can he show Cam that she isn't broken?

The Anchor Novels

Guarded Dreams — Eli & Ava

A grumpy-sunshine, military romance

He's a grumpy Coast Guard focused on his job. She's a feisty musician searching for stardom. Nothing about them fits, and yet their attraction burns wild when fate lands them in the same house for the summer.

Forged by Sacrifice — Mac & Georgie

A roommates-to-lovers, military romance

He's a driven military man zeroed in on a new goal. She's a struggling law student running from her family's mistakes. They're entirely wrong for each other…except their bodies disagree. When they end up as roommates, how long before attraction shatters their resistance?

Avenged by Love — Truck & Jersey

A fake-marriage, military romance

When a broody military man and a quiet bookstore clerk end up in the same house, it isn't only attraction that erupts. Now, the only way to ensure she gets the care she needs is to marry her.

Damaged Desires — Dani & Nash

A frenemy, military romance

A grumpy Navy SEAL reeling from the loss of his team fights an overwhelming attraction for his best friend's fiery sister, until a stalker puts her in his sights, and then he'll do anything to protect her, even if it means exposing all his secrets.

Branded by a Song — Brady & Tristan

A single-mom, rock star romance

He's a country-rock legend searching for inspiration. She's a Navy SEAL's widow determined to honor his memory while raising their daughter. Neither believes the intense attraction tugging at them can lead to more until their futures are twined by her grandmother's will.

Tripped by Love — Cassidy & Marco

A broody-bodyguard, single-mom romance

He's her brother's broody bodyguard with secrets he can't share. She's a busy single mom with a restaurant to run. They're just friends until a little white lie changes everything.

The Anchor Novels: The Military Bros Box Set

The books + an exclusive novella

Guarded Dreams, Forged by Sacrifice, and *Avenged by Love* plus the novella, *The Hurricane*! Heartfelt reads full of love, sacrifice, and family. The perfect book boyfriends for a binge read.

The Anchor Suspense Novels

Unmasked Dreams — Violet & Dawson

A second-chance, age-gap romance

Violet and Dawson had a heart-stopping attraction they were compelled to deny. When they're tossed together again, it proves nothing has changed—except the lab she's built in the garage and the secrets he's keeping. When she stumbles into his dark world, Dawson is forced to break old promises to keep her safe. But when the swells subside, will their hearts still be intact?

Crossed by the Stars — Jada & Dax

A second-chance, forced-proximity romance

Family secrets meant Dax and Jada's teenaged romance was an impossibility. A decade later, the scars still remain, so neither is willing to give in to their tantalizing chemistry. But when a shadow creeps out of Jada's past, seeking retribution, it's Dax who shows up to protect her. And suddenly, it's hard to see a way out without permanent damage to their bodies and souls.

Disguised as Love — Cruz & Raisa

A chemistry-filled, enemies-to-lovers romance

Surly FBI agent, Cruz Malone, is determined to bring down the Leskov clan for good. If that means he has to arrest or bed the sexy blonde scientist of the family, so be it. Too bad Raisa has other ideas. There's no way she's just going to sit back and let the infuriating agent dismantle her world…or her heart.

The Painted Daisies

Interconnected series with an all-female rock band, the alpha heroes who steal their hearts, and suspense that will leave you breathless. Each story has its own HEA.

Sweet Memory — Paisley & Jonas

An opposite-side-of-the-tracks, second-chance romance

The world's sweetest rock star falls for a troubled music producer whose past comes back to haunt them.

Green Jewel — Fiadh & Asher

An enemies-to-lovers, single-dad romance

He did it. She'll prove it. Her body's reaction to him be damned.

Cherry Brandy — Leya & Holden

A forced-proximity, forbidden, bodyguard romance

Being on the run with only one bed is no excuse to touch her…until touching is the only choice.

Blue Marguerite — Adria & Ronan

A celebrity, second-chance, frenemy romance

She vowed to never forgive him...not even when he offers answers her family desperately seeks.

Royal Haze — Nikki & D'Angelo

A bodyguard, on-the-run romance with a morally gray hero

He was ready to torture, steal, and kill to defend the world he believed in. What he wasn't prepared for...was her.

Free Stories

All available with a newsletter sign-up at
https://www.ljevansbooks.com/freeljbooks

Perfectly Fine

A fish-out-of-water, celebrity romance

He's a charming, A-list actor at the top of his game. She's a determined, small-town screenwriter hoping for a deal. They form an unexpected connection until heartbreak ruins their future. Also on Amazon.

Rumor

A small-town, rock-star romance

There's only one thing rock star Chase Legend needs to ring in the new year, and that's to know what Reyna Rossi tastes like. After ten years, there's no way he's letting her escape the night without their souls touching. Reyna has other plans. After all, she doesn't need the entire town wagging their tongues about her any more than they already do.

Love Ain't

A friends-to-lovers, cowboy romance

Reese knows her best friend and rodeo king, Dalton Abbott, is never going to fall in love, get married, and have kids. He's left so many broken hearts behind that there's gotta be a museum full of them somewhere. So when he gives her a look from under the brim of his hat, promising both jagged relief and pain, she knows better than to give in.

The Long Con

A sexy, antihero romance

Adler is after one thing: the next big payday. Then, Brielle sways into his world with her own game in play, and those aquamarine-colored eyes almost make him forget his number-one rule. But she'll learn... love isn't a con he's interested in.

The Light Princess

An old-fashioned fairy tale

A princess who glows with a magical light, a kingdom at war, and a kiss that changes the world. This is an extended version of the fairy tale twined through the pages of *Charming and the Cherry Blossom.*